MY NAME IS
COLEN

STEVE BARLOW AND STEVE SKIDMORE
Illustrated by SOPHIE ESCABASSE

TITLES AT THIS LEVEL

Fiction

978 1 4451 1812 3 pb

FISHING FOR
TROUBLE
DAVID AND HELEN ORME

978 1 4451 1811 6 pb

FOOTBALL
LEGEND
DAVID AND HELEN ORME

978 1 4451 1813 0 pb

VAMPIRES ARE
SO BORING
DAVID AND HELEN ORME

978 1 4451 3070 5 pb

MY NAME IS
COLEN
STEVE BARLOW AND STEVE SKIDMORE

978 1 4451 3054 5 pb

DEVIL'S
TEETH
STEVE BARLOW AND STEVE SKIDMORE

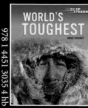
978 1 4451 3068 2 pb

SPACE
STATION ALERT
DAVID AND HELEN ORME

Graphic fiction

978 1 4451 1799 7 pb

DEMON
STREAK
JONNY ZUCKER AND STEVE SAMPSON

978 1 4451 1801 7 pb

FULL METAL
HERO
JONNY ZUCKER AND DAN BOULTWOOD

978 1 4451 1800 0 pb

TERROR
BEAST
JONNY ZUCKER AND JACK CHALKER

978 1 4451 3088 0 pb

ALIEN
ACADEMY
JONNY ZUCKER AND RYAN PENTNEY

978 1 4451 3090 3 pb

BEYOND THE
WALL
JONNY ZUCKER AND TOMAS ARANDA

978 1 4451 3089 7 pb

DOWNHILL
RACERS
JONNY ZUCKER AND IAIN McKMANN

Non-fiction

978 1 4451 1952 6 hb
978 1 4451 3229 7 pb

BIZARRE
BUILDINGS
ANNE ROONEY

978 1 4451 1954 0 hb
978 1 4451 3228 0 pb

CRAZY
FOOD
ANNE ROONEY

978 1 4451 1953 3 hb
978 1 4451 3227 3 pb

WACKY
SPORTS
ANNE ROONEY

978 1 4451 3050 7 hb

AMAZING
PETS
ANNE ROONEY

978 1 4451 3052 1 hb

DANGEROUS
EARTH
ANNE ROONEY

978 1 4451 3035 4 hb

WORLD'S
TOUGHEST
ANNE ROONEY

MY NAME IS
COLEN

STEVE BARLOW AND STEVE SKIDMORE
Illustrated by SOPHIE ESCABASSE

EDGE
FRANKLIN WATTS
LONDON·SYDNEY

First published in 2014 by
Franklin Watts
338 Euston Road
London NW1 3BH

Franklin Watts Australia
Level 17/207 Kent Street
Sydney NSW 2000

A CIP catalogue record for this book is
available from the British Library.

(pb) ISBN: 978 1 4451 3070 5
(library ebook) ISBN: 978 1 4451 3071 2

Series Editors: Adrian Cole and Jackie Hamley
Series Advisors: Diana Bentley and Dee Reid
Series Designer: Peter Scoulding

1 3 5 7 9 10 8 6 4 2

Printed in China

Franklin Watts is a division of
Hachette Children's Books,
an Hachette UK company.
www.hachette.co.uk

CONTENTS

CHAPTER 1

A NEW NEIGHBOUR

Becca was helping her parents carry boxes into their new home.

The house next door was old and spooky.

Becca looked up and saw a boy watching her from a window.

Next morning, Becca saw the boy in the garden.

"Hi," she said. "I'm Becca."

"I'm Colen," said the boy.

Becca laughed. "Did you say 'Colin'?"

"My name is Colen with an e," said the boy,
"not Colin with an i."

Becca grinned. "Maybe we will be in the same class at school."

"I don't go to school," said Colen. "Uncle John teaches me at home."

"Well, maybe we could hang out," said Becca.

"I never go out," said Colen.

CHAPTER 2
UNCLE JOHN

Becca stared at Colen. "Don't your parents take you out?"

"They died so Uncle John brought me up," said Colen. "He's a scientist and he has a big lab upstairs..."

"What's going on?" said a stern voice.

Colen looked scared.

"This is Uncle John," he said.

"Hello," said Becca. "We have just moved in next door. I hope Colen and I can be friends..."

"Colen doesn't need friends," said Uncle John.

"Go into the house," said Uncle John to Colen.

Then he stared at Becca.
"Stay away from Colen!"

Becca was angry, but she was surprised too. Colen and his Uncle John looked so like each other.

CHAPTER 3

A REBELLION

When they were inside their house,

Colen spoke crossly to Uncle John.

"Why did you say that to Becca?" he asked.

"Why can't I have friends?"

"That will do, Colen," said Uncle John.

Colen headed for the door. "I'm going out,"
he said.

"I don't think so," said Uncle John.

"You can't stop me!" said Colen.

"Can't I?" said Uncle John.

CHAPTER 4
THE SWITCH

Colen was strapped to a chair.

"You never had any parents," said Uncle John.
"I cloned you from my own cells. That's why
I named you Colen – 'Clone' with the letters
changed. You are an exact copy of me."

"My heart is weak, so I will transfer my mind into your body," said Uncle John. "I will become you and I shall be young again!"

CHAPTER 5
A CHANGE OF MIND

Next day, Colen called for Becca. "Let's go out," he said.

"But what about Uncle John?" said Becca.

"We don't need to worry about him," said Colen. "He went away."

"Let's go and see a film," said Becca.

"Sounds good," said Uncle John.

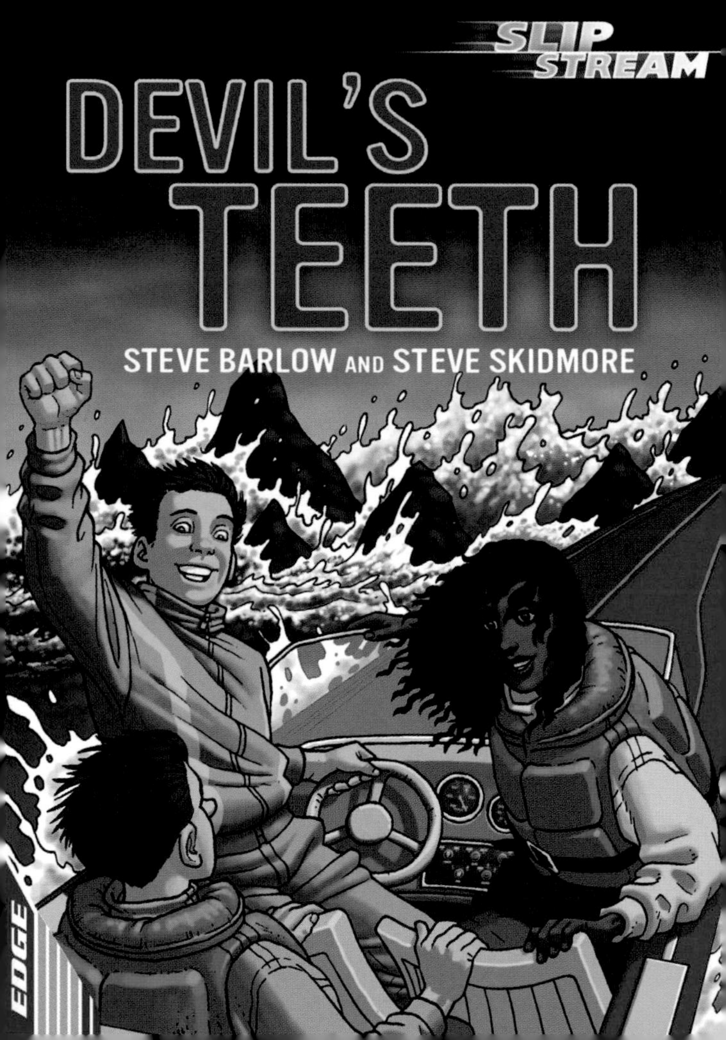
SLIP STREAM
DEVIL'S TEETH
STEVE BARLOW AND STEVE SKIDMORE
EDGE

When Owen agrees to go for a trip with Emma on Jeb's boat, he has no idea how reckless Jeb will be. Now a storm is coming and they are dangerously close to the Devil's Teeth rocks. How can Owen get them back to shore alive?

LONDON•SYDNEY

Space station duty can be boring. But when a direct hit causes
the air supply to fail, Chris and Rob are definitely not bored.
Ground control has been hit by a hurricane so there's no help
on the way from Earth, and they have just 12 hours to try to
save themselves...

LONDON·SYDNEY

About SLIP STREAM

Slipstream is a series of expertly levelled books designed for pupils who are struggling with reading. Its unique three-strand approach through fiction, graphic fiction and non-fiction gives pupils a rich reading experience that will accelerate their progress and close the reading gap.

At the heart of every Slipstream fiction book is a great story. Easily accessible words and phrases ensure that pupils both decode and comprehend, and the high interest stories really engage older struggling readers.

Whether you're using Slipstream Level 2 for Guided Reading or as an independent read, here are some suggestions:

1. Make each reading session successful. Talk about the text before the pupil starts reading. Introduce any unfamiliar vocabulary.

2. Encourage the pupil to talk about the book using a range of open questions. For example, who would be the best next door neighbour? Who would be the worst?

3. Discuss the differences between reading fiction, graphic fiction and non-fiction. Which do they prefer?

For guidance, SLIPSTREAM Level 2 – My Name is Colen has been approximately measured to:

National Curriculum Level: 2b
Reading Age: 7.6–8.0
Book Band: Purple

ATOS: 2.1*
Guided Reading Level: I
Lexile® Measure (confirmed): 320L

*Please check actual Accelerated Reader™ book level and quiz availability at www.arbookfind.co.uk